Katy's Exmoor Adventures

The Sequel to Katy's Exmoor

By Victoria Eveleigh

Illustrated by Chris Eveleigh

We would like to thank all those who helped and
encouraged us in the production of this book.
Particular thanks to Sally Chapman-Walker for designing
the book, and Marcia Monbleau and Sue Croft
for their advice.

Photograph of Chris and Victoria Eveleigh by Guy Harrop.
Photograph of Exmoor ponies by Pam Sydenham.

In writing this story, every attempt has been made to make
it true to Exmoor by using local names, while avoiding the
use of specific names of people and farms known to the
author. The characters in this story are fictitious, and any
resemblance to real people is purely coincidental.

First published in 2003 by Tortoise Publishing
This edition published in 2006 by Tortoise Publishing

ISBN 978 0 9542021 1 8

Printed in Great Britain by Toptown Printers Limited,
Vicarage Lawn, Barnstaple, North Devon EX32 7BN

Book Design by Sally Chapman-Walker

Published and distributed by
Tortoise Publishing,
West Ilkerton Farm,
Lynton, Exmoor,
North Devon EX35 6QA
Tel/Fax (01598) 752310
Email info@tortoise-publishing.co.uk
Website www.tortoise-publishing.co.uk

This book is dedicated to
Anne and Paddy,
my mother and father.

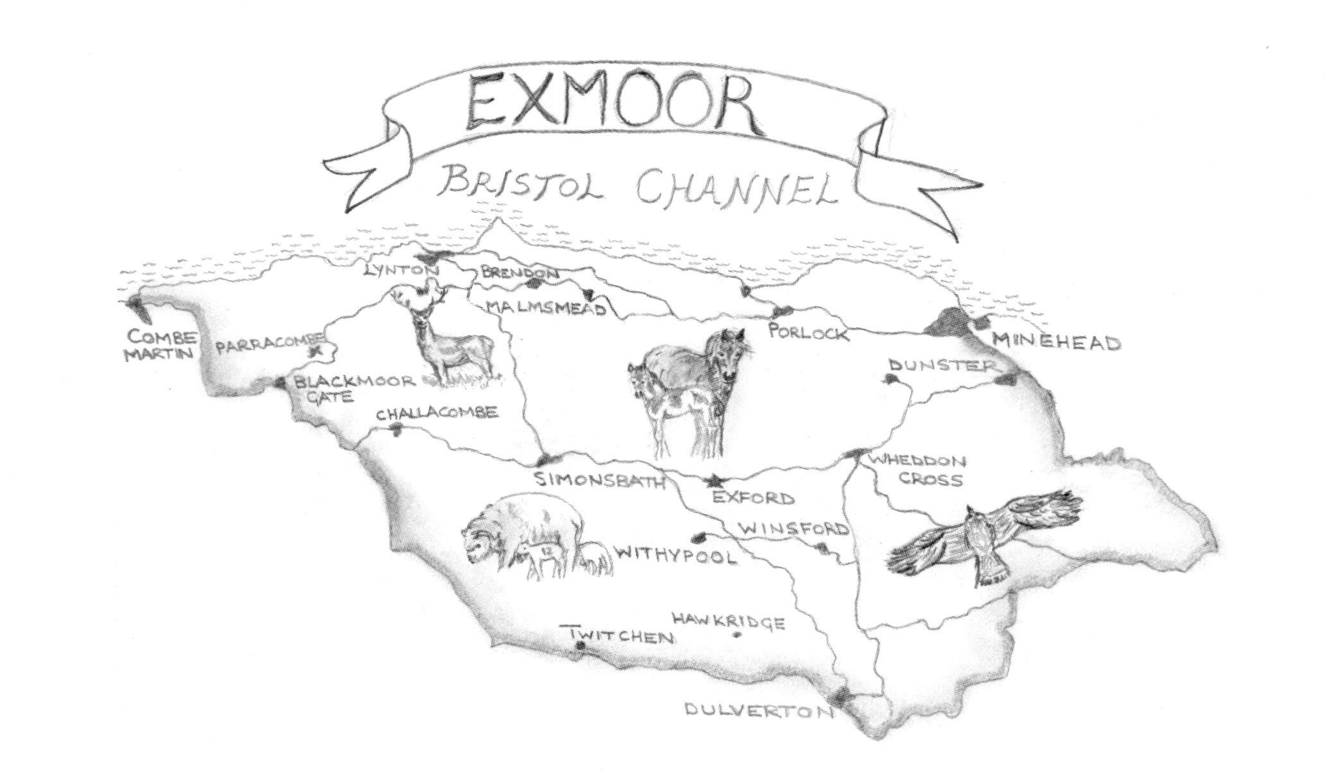
EXMOOR
BRISTOL CHANNEL
LYNTON
BRENDON
MALMSMEAD
PORLOCK
MINEHEAD
COMBE MARTIN
PARRACOMBE
BLACKMOOR GATE
CHALLACOMBE
DUNSTER
WHEDDON CROSS
SIMONSBATH
EXFORD
WINSFORD
WITHYPOOL
HAWKRIDGE
TWITCHEN
DULVERTON

Katy's Exmoor Adventures

Contents

Auld Lang Syne

Should auld acquaintance be forgot,
And never brought to mind?
Should auld acquaintance be forgot,
And auld lang syne?
For auld lang syne, my dear,
For auld lang syne,
We'll tak a cup of kindness yet,
For the sake of auld lang syne.

Chapter 1

Times Gone By

The evening of the last day of the 20th century was unremarkable. It was a typical Exmoor winter's evening — chilly but not really cold, and drizzly but not really raining.

Katy Squires and her best friend, Alice, stood in the old cow shed which had been converted into stabling for Katy's two ponies at her home, Barton Farm. The girls leaned on the stable wall inside the shed and chatted easily as they watched the ponies eat their hay. Jacko was a sleek, liver chestnut gelding. He was 13.2 hands high, ten years old, dependable, experienced and lovely to ride. Trifle was a yearling registered Exmoor filly who still had a lot to learn. She had been born on the moor above Barton Farm on Katy's ninth birthday. Trifle's thick winter coat made her look like a life-sized cuddly toy.

Trifle and Jacko had been together at Barton for nearly a year now, and Katy couldn't imagine life without them. She looked at the contented ponies, breathed in the wonderful stable smell and felt pure happiness envelop her like a warm blanket.

"Have you made any New Year's resolutions, then?" Alice asked.

"Mmmm. I suppose I ought to," said Katy. "I'd like to eat fewer sweets and win lots of rosettes. Oh yes, and I want Trifle to become a champion Exmoor pony."

"Are those wishes or resolutions? A resolution is something you're going to do, not something you wish would happen."

Katy gave her friend a light punch on the arm. "Oh, you're such a know-it-all, Alice Gardener! They're a bit of both, I suppose. So what are your resolutions, clever-clogs?"

"OK. My resolution is to try to be nice to my terrible twin brothers, and my wish is that I'll be happy at my new school after I leave Lynton Primary in the summer."

"I shouldn't worry about that, Alice. Everybody at school likes you, and we'll all be going on to Ilfracombe College together," Katy replied.

"Um, I've been meaning to tell you this, Katy."

Katy was unconcerned. "Well, tell me quickly because we'd better go and get ready for the party."

"I'm not going to Ilfracombe with you," Alice blurted out.

"What do you mean? You can't stop going to school yet, you know."

"I know that, silly. I'm going to a different school. A boarding school miles away."

"Oh, Alice! Poor you! How awful!"

"No, you don't understand. I want to go. It looks like a really cool place. They do loads of games, and you can even take your own pony. I'm really looking forward to it. I wish you could come too, though. We'd have a wicked time together, wouldn't we?"

Katy was close to tears. "Well, thanks for rubbing it in!"

Alice looked bewildered. "Rubbing what in?"

"You know that my mum and dad would never be able to afford a boarding school! They're not rich like your family!" Tears started to run down Katy's cheeks. She turned and ran out of the shed.

"Katy! Please come back! I didn't mean it like that!" Alice called after her.

Katy knew Alice hadn't meant to be thoughtless. What really hurt was that Alice could imagine having a good time at a new school without her. The thought of going to Ilfracombe without Alice was dreadful.

"Shut up, Alice! I'm not listening!" Katy shouted into the damp night.

The Millennium party was in Lynton Town Hall. There was a barn dance for all ages, with a band and a caller who told everyone what they should be doing. Some people knew the steps already and others got in terrible muddles, but everyone had a good time. It was impossible for Katy to be sulky in that kind of atmosphere. She and Alice were soon together again, talking and dancing as if the conversation earlier in the evening had never happened.

"Take your partners for The West Country Waltz!" the caller announced.

"Let's sit this one out. It sounds complicated, and I'm done in!" Katy said to Alice.

They went back to the table where Katy's Gran and Granfer were sitting chatting to Phil and Sally, Katy's father and mother.

Katy collapsed onto a chair in a mock faint. "We're shattered!" she announced.

"Pah!" Granfer scoffed. "Young people don't have any stamina nowadays! Come on, Peggy love, we'd better show them how it's done!"

To Katy's horror, Granfer took Gran's hand and led her onto the dance floor.

"How embarrassing!" Katy whispered to Alice, but her embarrassment soon turned into amazement.

Gran and Granfer danced gracefully and in perfect harmony, their feet hardly touching the floor. The other dancers stood and watched in awe as the couple swept round the room with breathtaking style.

"I had no idea Granfer could dance like that, and how does Gran manage with her arthritis?" Katy asked her father.

"When Gran gets her dancing shoes on, nothing stops her," Phil answered. "Gran and Granfer used to win all sorts of prizes for their dancing when they were younger. The money they won helped them to turn Barton into one of the best farms on Exmoor."

For the first time, Katy imagined her Gran and Granfer as a handsome young couple with their whole lives in front of them, long before they were 'Gran' and 'Granfer' or even 'Mum' and 'Dad'.

The dance finished, and everybody burst into applause.

In no time at all it was nearly midnight. There was a hush as someone tuned in a radio and plugged it into the sound system. Big Ben struck 12, and everyone was hugging and kissing and saying, "Happy New Millennium!" Then they formed a huge circle, held hands with crossed arms and sang 'Auld Lang Syne'.

Katy was sandwiched between Alice and Granfer, diving in and out of the circle in a long, snake-like chain as they sang the chorus.

"What on earth does 'auld lang syne' mean?" Katy asked Granfer as she and Alice giggled about the words afterwards.

"Roughly translated, it means 'times gone by'," Granfer explained. "It's a Scottish song but it's become traditional to sing it on New Year's Eve in England, too. We were singing 'we'll drink to old friends and times gone by', and that's just what we're going to do. Follow me, ladies!"

Granfer, Katy and Alice went back to the table where Gran was sitting. Granfer handed the girls their drinks, raised his glass of beer and said, "To auld lang syne!"

"To auld lang syne!" the girls repeated, giggling. Katy took a sip of lemonade, and the bubbles went up her nose.

The Squires family got home from the party in the early hours of the morning. Gran and Granfer stayed at Barton Farm for the night so they did not have to drive back to their bungalow in Porlock. Sally had not taken in any bed and breakfast guests that night.

Two members of the family had not been at the party in Lynton: Tom and Rachel. Tom was Katy's 19-year-old brother. He was at Bicton Agricultural College, and had spent the New Year with friends in Bideford. Auntie Rachel was Phil's younger sister, and was more like an older sister than an aunt to Katy. Rachel and her boyfriend, Mark, had gone to a party at the pub in Simonsbath. Rachel worked at a hunter livery yard in Exford, and Mark lived with his family on a farm near Simonsbath.

Sally had just finished cooking breakfast in the kitchen when the telephone rang.

Phil sat eating his eggs and bacon. "My New Year's resolution is to not answer the telephone at meal times. I'm fed up with ruined meals because of the damned phone," he complained. "Who on earth could be ringing at this ..."

Sally gestured to him to be quiet as she answered the telephone.

"Barton Farm. Can I help you? Oh! Hello, Rachel. Happy New Year to you, too. What? Well, that's marvellous news! Congratulations! I'm thrilled for you both. Jack and Peggy are here, so do you want a quick word? We'll see you soon. OK. Love and congratulations to Mark. Bye, now."

Granfer went to the telephone with a heavy heart. He had guessed what the call was about, and he was not particularly happy. He had hoped for someone better than Mark for his wonderful only daughter.

"Hello, Rachel love. Well done. I expect you want to speak to Mum, then. Yes, you too. Take care, now."

Gran took the telephone from Granfer and settled down for a long chat. While she was talking on the telephone the rest of the family talked in whispers.

"You were a bit short with her, Jack," Sally scolded.

"I'm sorry, but I can't pretend I'm something that I'm not, and I'm not happy about this," Granfer replied.

"Not happy about what?" Katy asked, forgetting to whisper.

"Ssshhhh!" Granfer, Phil and Sally hissed together.

"There's too much noise in here, Rachel. I'll just change to the telephone in the hall. Hang on a minute," Gran said, giving the family one of her stern looks.

With Gran talking behind a closed door in the hall, everyone talked more normally in the kitchen, although they were secretly trying to eavesdrop on Gran's conversation at the same time.

"Rachel and Mark are engaged to be married," Sally explained to Katy.

"More's the pity," added Granfer.

"Oh, come on, Dad! She could do a lot worse! The trouble is that nobody would be good enough for Rachel in your eyes," Phil said.

"That's not true. Now, if she were going to marry Mark's brother, Greg, that would be a different matter altogether. He's a proper worker, he is." As far as Granfer was concerned to be a good worker was the most important quality in a man, closely followed by honesty. "Mark always does as little as possible on his own farm, and he never helps on ours. He's like a blister: he shows up when all the work is done."

They all started to laugh, but they fell silent as the tone of Gran's voice in the hall changed.

"You're what? You can't be! When? That soon?"

Gran came back into the kitchen, looking as white as a sheet. "Oh, Jack! Rachel says that they can't see a future here on Exmoor. If hunting is banned, she'll be out of a job, and Mark doesn't want to take on the farm at Simonsbath with agriculture in the state it's in. He's got an uncle who's offered him a good job and so ..."

"Thank goodness for that. At least he'll be working, then," Granfer interrupted.

"Just listen to me for once, you old fool!" Gran snapped unexpectedly. "They're going to Australia!"

What a lot of things had happened in 24 hours, Katy thought as she put the ponies out in the field later that morning. She watched as they galloped off together without a care in the world. Alice had promised to be her best friend forever, and Rachel had promised to help her break-in

Trifle, but they had either forgotten or didn't care. Both Alice and Rachel had made different plans for the future, and Katy was no part of them. The words of 'Auld Lang Syne' came swimming into her head again. They weren't funny any more, just sad. It seemed that the song had hidden messages about how people move on and friendships fade away. How on earth was she going to cope without Alice and Auntie Rachel?

Chapter 2

Moon

Rachel was a very gifted horsewoman: many horses with seemingly impossible problems had been cured by her at a fraction of the price which she should have charged, considering the value she added to the horses by working with them. She would be missed by many people — and horses — when she went to Australia.

The horse who would miss her most was her own. He was a six-year-old Thoroughbred named New Moon because he was dark bay except for a white marking like a new moon between his eyes. In the middle of the moon there was a perfectly placed large whorl of hair. Moon had been sent to Rachel as a last resort because he attacked anyone who came within biting distance. Rachel loved all horses, but there was something extra-special about Moon. The horse knew he could trust Rachel, and soon he was greeting her with pricked ears and a whinny rather than snapping teeth. Rachel kept him for much longer than she needed to because she couldn't bear to let him go. She had never before ridden a horse of such quality and intelligence.

Eventually, and with a heavy heart, Rachel had contacted the owner. He came to get Moon, brandishing a long whip to use on the horse if he misbehaved. Moon took one look at the whip and decided attack was the best form of defence. The owner refused to pay Rachel the £150 he owed her. He said he was taking the horse directly to the abattoir to be destroyed, so Rachel saved him the journey and bought Moon for £500. Within a year, Rachel and Moon had won many prizes in local competitions, and Moon had become one of the best hunters on Exmoor. He was beautiful, fast, sure-footed and sensible, and he would do anything for Rachel. Moon was Rachel's horse of a lifetime.

Word soon got around that Rachel was going to Australia. A wealthy retired businessman called Mr. Jackson, who lived near Winsford, was looking for a good hunter. He offered Rachel £6,000 for Moon. It was an offer she couldn't refuse. She banked the cheque, but felt like a traitor.

Chapter 3

Early Learning

It was hard to be enthusiastic about riding in the middle of winter, especially on school days. Katy arrived home just before 4 o'clock every day. She had to muck out the stables, catch and groom the ponies, ride Jacko and give Trifle a leading lesson — all before darkness fell. If it was raining or very frosty, she often skipped the riding and leading parts of her routine, and then felt guilty. When she had longed for a pony of her own, she imagined spending every waking moment with it. Now, she was lucky enough to have two ponies, but sometimes she found it difficult to be enthusiastic when it was cold and wet outside.

It was different when Rachel came over to help, which she did quite often that winter. Rachel had remembered her promise to Katy, and was very sorry that she would not be around to help when Trifle was old enough to be ridden. Still, she could help with a lot of essential groundwork before going to Australia. Trifle and Katy both learnt a great deal from Rachel, often learning the most when things went wrong.

On a frosty evening in January, Rachel stood in the paddock at Barton with Katy and a very impatient Trifle who was eager to join Jacko in the stable.

"Remember, Katy, the boss horse controls other horses in the herd by moving them around. To control a horse, you have to be able to control its movements. If Trifle decides to go forwards — like she did then — make her go back to where she started. Teaching a horse to stand still is really important. Don't let her move until you say so."

"Easier said than done!" Katy mumbled as she pushed into Trifle's shoulder to make her go backwards. Trifle sidestepped and tried to give Katy a playful nip. Without thinking, Katy slapped Trifle on the nose in self-defence. Trifle shot backwards with her head in the air, nearly pulling Katy off her feet. Katy's hands were cold — even with gloves on — and the sudden tug of the rope hurt terribly. "Ow! Stop it!" she yelled at Trifle, pulling down hard on the rope and glaring into the pony's eyes.

Trifle took fright at this unexpected aggression from a person she usually trusted. She pulled away, hurting Katy's hands again, and kicked out sideways as she wheeled round. Then she galloped round the paddock, slipping on the frozen ground and tripping on the trailing rope.

"Well, what have you just learnt?" Rachel asked calmly.

"That I'd rather be inside watching television," Katy replied truthfully.

In fact, Katy learnt a great deal that evening. Rachel caught Trifle and worked with her while Katy watched and listened. There was something in Rachel's quiet, confident manner which made the pony pay attention and concentrate. With the slightest of body movements, Rachel made Trifle go forwards, backwards and in circles.

"I hope you see why I told you to wear gloves and a hard hat," Rachel said as she worked. "Bangs on the head aren't a good idea, and it's difficult to stay calm when all of the skin has been ripped off your hands. Well done for not having the rope wrapped around your hand; that could have been nasty. I remember Phil being dragged across a field by his pony because he had the rope looped around his hand and couldn't free himself. He was badly hurt but your Granfer still gave him the most awful ticking-off. Poor Phil! He really didn't have much luck with ponies. Now then, do you see what I am doing here? I'm putting pressure on the halter using the rope, but as soon as Trifle responds by doing what I ask, I release the pressure and that is her reward. If you don't release the pressure at the moment that she does the right thing, there's no reward for her and you'll make her confused and unsure of what you want. Then it's a downward spiral because you'll have to use more and more pressure to get a response. Come and have a go yourself now, Katy."

Trifle did exactly as Katy asked. "She just didn't understand what I wanted before, did she? She follows my every move now," Katy said, smiling.

"The same principle will apply when you start riding Trifle. Exmoor ponies are very intelligent and you can make them sulky very easily if you nag them or treat them unfairly." She stroked Trifle's forehead. "We don't want that, do we sweetheart?"

Katy was shivering with cold. “Brrr! I’m getting so frozen that my feet are nearly dropping off. Do you mind if we go in now?”

“No, that’s OK. I was going to stop now, anyway. It’s a good idea to keep lessons with young horses short, and always end on a good note. Don’t worry when things go wrong. They often do, but the great thing is to put them right, like we did today.”

“Like you did today, you mean!” Katy replied. “How am I going to ride Trifle without your help?”

“You’ll manage. We’re doing the important training now. She’ll be a doddle,” Rachel said confidently.

“May I have that in writing?” Katy asked, sounding much more light-hearted than she felt.

Chapter 4

Spring

On April 1st, Trifle was two years old and Katy was eleven. They celebrated their shared birthday by giving the family a display of the skills which Trifle and Katy had learnt since the New Year. Alice and Melanie — Alice's mother — came over to watch, too. Melanie was very fond of Katy and Trifle. She had kept Trifle at Stonyford, her riding stables, when the pony was a newly-weaned foal. Melanie could still remember her as a scrawny, frightened, un-handled foal. The change was truly amazing.

Trifle was led, long-reined, backed through poles, and trotted over a very small jump. She walked over some black plastic silage-wrap and stood still on a marked spot for a minute. When she and Katy had finished, everyone clapped. Trifle had never heard clapping before. She shot backwards in alarm, but Katy managed to hang on to the rope.

"You'll have to get her used to clapping and loud noises before you take her to shows, you know," Granfer said. "You know the saying, don't you?" He continued before anyone could answer, "An amateur practises until he gets it right. A professional practises until he can't get it wrong."

"Well in that case, you'd better start practising being a bridesmaid, Katy. I certainly don't want any amateur bridesmaids at my wedding," Rachel said.

"Wicked! You want me to be your bridesmaid?" Katy exclaimed.

"If you can put up with wearing a dress and walking down the aisle with Greg, who's going to be Mark's best man," Rachel replied.

Katy blushed. Alice was making embarrassing swooning gestures, but luckily no one else noticed. Mark was the oldest of four brothers;

there was a gap of sixteen years between Mark and his youngest brother, Greg, but the two brothers were very close. Katy had worshipped Greg from afar ever since he had come over to help with haymaking two years before. Since then, he had often helped out with jobs around the farm. The thought of walking down the aisle with Greg was like a dream come true. "I think I could put up with that," she said coolly.

That April was the wettest in England and Wales since records began in 1766. It was very wet and unusually cold. During the last two weeks of lambing at Barton, a great deal of snow fell. After an awful blizzard, Phil found 24 dead lambs and a dead cow. By the end of the month, everyone at Barton Farm was exhausted and depressed. Phil had to visit his bank manager and arrange for the farm overdraft to be increased, yet again. At night, he often lay awake worrying about money until he felt physically sick. Because Phil dealt with the farm accounts, the other members of the family were blissfully unaware of the farm's problems. They were just glad that the twin nightmares of lambing and the awful weather were over, and they looked forward to Rachel's wedding in May.

Chapter 5
The Wedding

The wedding service was held at Exford Church because Rachel sang in the choir there and had lots of friends in the area.

It was a perfect wedding. The weather was sunny and clear, nobody was late or ill and, best of all, Greg actually linked arms with Katy to walk down the aisle. Katy walked as slowly as she could to make the moment last as long as possible. A carriage pulled by a pair of grey Shire horses took the bride and groom from the church down the hill to the hotel in Exford where the reception was held.

The same band which had played at the Millennium party was there, and soon everyone was up and dancing. Greg asked Katy to dance. She knew that he was 20, and he had a stunning girlfriend who had probably told him to dance with the bridesmaid, but Katy didn't care. She had two dances with Greg, and then the caller announced The West Country Waltz. Katy heard a familiar voice.

"May I have the pleasure of this dance?" It was Granfer.

"How about Gran?" Katy asked.

"She wants to sit down. It's been a long day."

Katy was panic-stricken. "But I don't know what to do, Granfer. I can't dance properly like you can."

"No such word as 'can't'," Granfer replied, guiding her to the centre of the dance floor. "Just let me do the steering, OK? When I move, you move with me."

"A bit like training Trifle," Katy giggled.

"Exactly!"

Katy would remember that dance all her life. Granfer literally swept her off her feet. Her long, sky-blue, silk bridesmaid's dress swirled around her as she danced, and she felt very grown-up. It was so fantastic to dance with a person who knew exactly what he was doing, especially when that person was her wonderful Granfer. It was only when the music stopped that Katy realised they had cleared the dance floor and everybody was clapping.

"Do you always clear the floor when you dance?" Katy asked Granfer.

Granfer smiled mischievously. "Only when people are afraid that the woman I'm dancing with will tread on their toes!" he replied.

Rachel and Mark gave Katy a silver photo frame as a present for being their bridesmaid. There were three windows for pictures. Katy chose her best photos of Trifle and Jacko to put in two of the windows, and one of Rachel on Moon to put in the third.

On the day before Rachel and Mark left for Australia, they went to Barton for a farewell tea. Afterwards, all the family gathered outside to say their goodbyes.

Granfer kissed Rachel and said softly in her ear, "I'm letting you go only if you promise to swallow your pride and come back home if you're unhappy." Then he raised his voice. "Have a safe journey, then, Rachel love. Good luck." He turned to Mark but couldn't look him in the eye.

"Take care of her," he said, and then he hurried indoors before anyone could see that he was crying.

Katy hugged Rachel. "Thanks for all your help, Rachel. I'll miss you so much."

"Not half as much as I'll miss you. Take care of yourself and that cheeky little pony of yours. Oh, and Katy, try to look out for Moon, will you? He's with Mr. Jackson over at Winsford. Let me know how he gets on."

Chapter 6

Ride Across Exmoor

Melanie had an idea while she was in the bath, which turned into a plan, which turned into a three-day holiday of a lifetime for Alice and Katy.

When she was a girl, Melanie's family had taken riding holidays on Exmoor. They had hired horses from stables near Timberscombe. The memory of those idyllic times had inspired Melanie to buy a riding school on Exmoor after she divorced Alice's father. For the past two years, she had been so busy getting Stonyford Riding Stables up and running that she had not spent enough time with her children. However, now she had Penny — their very good groom and mother's help at Stonyford — and Melanie was sure she would be able to get extra help for a few days during the summer. The time was right to show her children Exmoor, the magical kingdom they were living in but were always too busy to explore. Katy could come, too. She would be good company for Alice, and it would give the two friends a special time together before they went to different schools in the autumn.

Melanie, Alice, Katy and the twins, Josh and Rupert, set off from Stonyford in blazing sunshine. The rucksacks on their backs and the head collars under their horses' bridles added to the exciting feeling that they were starting out on a great expedition. By the time they reached Dry Bridge on Brendon Common, black clouds had blotted out the sun. As they crossed the river by the deserted village at Badgworthy Lees, heavy drops of rain began to fall. Josh and Rupert, who had wanted to gallop all the way to begin with, now lagged behind and complained bitterly that they were cold, wet, bored, hungry, aching and a lot more besides. Melanie started to regret bringing them.

They were approaching the ruined farmstead at Larkbarrow when the heavens opened and there was a spectacular thunderstorm. Hailstones like billions of white frozen peas crashed to the ground and covered everything in a slippery layer of ice. They stung the ponies and made them prance around. Josh started to scream and his pony took fright and bolted, with Rupert's pony following hot on his heels. Melanie swore and went after them. Alice and Katy tried to shelter by a broken down wall.

"Well, they did say that they wanted a gallop!" Alice said heartlessly.

"You are horrible to your brothers, Alice!" Katy exclaimed. Her shaky voice betrayed how frightened she was.

"You would be too if you had to live with them," Alice said. "This is an odd place, isn't it? Mum was saying that it was a proper farm right up to the Second World War when the family was evacuated because the army wanted to use the area for target practice. You can see lots of holes in these walls. Look."

"How awful!" Katy exclaimed. 'I can't imagine what it must be like to lose your home like that! Thank goodness that sort of thing doesn't happen now. One thing's for certain, the Squires family will never leave Barton. I wonder how the boys are; I do hope they're OK."

At that moment, three riders came round the corner. Melanie was leading Josh and Rupert, and both boys were sobbing.

"Miraculously, we're all in one piece!" Melanie said with false jollity. She looked very shaken.

Soon, the storm blew over, and the bedraggled party made its way over the boggy ground to Alderman's Barrow and then across Almsworthy Common to Hillhead Cross. From there, it was a short ride down into Exford village. The sun was surprisingly hot when it did come out, and the riders and ponies steamed like boiling kettles.

When they reached Exford, Melanie told the girls that Josh and Rupert had decided they wanted to go home. Penny could come over and collect them in the morning, and Melanie would continue the holiday with Alice and Katy.

Katy had never stayed in a hotel before. It was so smart and luxurious. The two girls shared a twin-bedded room complete with their own bathroom.

The horses had a top-class hotel, too. The boxes at Exford Stables were large, old-fashioned, immaculate and built around a central courtyard so the horses could see each other. Some hunters were back from their summer rest to get fit for the start of the season, but many of the boxes were empty. Moon's old loosebox was empty, and the girl who had replaced Rachel was grumpy. The place felt different without Rachel, and Katy missed her terribly.

After the twins left for Stonyford the next morning, the girls set off with Melanie, under a dull, grey, warm blanket of light mist. They crossed the River Exe and followed the bridle path towards Winsford. Soon they were in a steep-sided valley where the mist swirled around them. The slopes of the valley were covered in bracken and gnarled trees.

"Don't those trees look like little old men, looming out of the mist like that?" Katy said, shivering slightly. "Granfer told me about the ghost of the highwayman, Tom Faggus, riding his faithful mare, Winnie. You can't hear him because Winnie's shoes are muffled with leather boots and ..."

"Katy! Shut up!" said Alice

"Now, now, girls!" Melanie said quickly. "It's such a pity that the weather's closed in on us, because this is a really beautiful valley."

"That's what Mum is always saying to her guests when she takes them riding in the pouring rain!" Alice said.

A short way down the valley, Alice's sharp eyes spotted a dark shape in a clump of bracken. It was a red deer calf.

"Oh, it's adorable!" exclaimed Alice. "Do you think it's been abandoned? Perhaps we should take it with us and find a vet or somebody to take care of it. Will you hold my pony, Katy, so I can go and stroke it?"

"Um, I don't think that's a good idea, Alice," Katy replied. "Granfer told me that a hind will hide her calf in an overgrown place like that while she goes off to graze. I bet that the hind isn't too far away and she knows exactly where her calf is."

"Quite right, Katy," Melanie agreed. "We can look at it from a safe distance instead."

The grey silhouette of a hind appeared on the misty hill above the riders. She hesitated when she saw them and then started to move away. They moved on quickly in case she was the mother of the calf.

Soon they reached a lane, which ran past two farms and over a bridge, and joined the road a mile or so outside Winsford. As they started to ride down the road, Jacko's hoof beats sounded rather odd.

"Typical!" Melanie said, sighing, "Jacko's got a loose shoe. That's all we need!"

"But he was shod only a short while ago!" Katy protested.

"If Jacko's got a fault it's that he has very soft hooves," Melanie replied. "It means that shoes get loose on him pretty quickly, especially if he's had a lot of work."

Katy was terribly disappointed. It looked as if her riding holiday would be cut short, too.

Melanie tried to be positive. "I'll see if I can find a farrier when we get to Winsford, but don't get your hopes too high."

They were riding past a smart-looking house with a beautiful garden. Beyond the house was a modern stable yard right next to the road. A horse and a small pony were standing in the yard. A tall, grey-haired gentleman was brushing the horse.

"That horse looks like Moon!" Katy exclaimed.

The gentleman came over to greet the riders, his hand raised in a welcoming gesture. Katy and Alice had been amazed at the friendly greetings they had received from total strangers all over Exmoor, just because they were riding.

"Did I hear you say that you know Moon?" the gentleman asked.

Katy blushed. "Oh dear, is my voice that loud? My Auntie Rachel sold him to you, didn't she?"

"She did indeed! So you must be Katy. What a pleasure to meet you!"

"I'm really glad to meet you, too. I promised that I'd look out for Moon, you see."

"Well, you'd better come on in and give him a thorough inspection then, my girl. Good lord, I'm forgetting my manners! The name's Jackson — John Jackson," he said, reaching up to shake Melanie's hand. "Why don't you all tie up your horses and come in for a cup of coffee or whatever, eh?"

Melanie hesitated in her reply. "Er, Mr. Jackson. That's ... "

"Oh, please! Call me John."

"Um, John, that's very kind of you, but I think we'd better press on. Katy's pony has a loose shoe and we've got to find a farrier as quickly as possible. Do you know of anyone who could come out at short notice?"

Mr. Jackson smiled in the direction of a Landrover, which had turned into the drive and was heading towards the stables. "Well, that's what I call service!" he remarked.

The Landrover stopped and a short, wiry man got out. "Morning, Mr. Jackson, Sir."

"Good morning, Peter. This young lady was wondering if I knew of a farrier who could fix her pony's loose shoe. Can you think of anyone?"

"That's a tough one, Sir. The man I have in mind will do anything for a nice cup of coffee."

"I'd better put the kettle on, then," Mr. Jackson replied. He turned to the riders and smiled. "Bring your horses in and tie them up over there. Peter has come to shoe Moon. He'll tap the pony's shoe on for you, no problem."

"Oh, thank you, Mr. Jackson! You've saved our holiday!" Katy exclaimed.

"Don't thank me, thank Peter," Mr. Jackson replied, smiling. " Now then, young lady, come and see Moon."

Moon looked fantastic. He was fat with summer grass and obviously very happy and relaxed.

"I keep Tinkerbell, the pony, for the grand-children, you know. Moon and Tinks are firm friends, aren't you, eh?" He stroked Moon's neck gently as he spoke. "Right then, refreshments are called for. Follow me, girls. One coffee coming up, Peter!"

Mrs. Jackson was a good-looking, plump, motherly lady. She insisted that she should make sandwiches for them all, as it was nearly lunchtime. By the time they'd eaten, the farrier had finished. "All done and ready to go," he said cheerfully.

"Thank you so much. How much do I owe you?" Melanie asked.

"I won't hear of it! Put it on my bill, Peter, there's a good chap." Mr Jackson said firmly.

"Oh, it's much too kind of you."

"Not another word! It's my pleasure!" said Mr Jackson. "So nice to see the young enjoying themselves properly. None of this addiction to the goggle box which seems to plague so many children these days."

Katy and Alice smiled knowingly at each other. Katy's mum had been left with strict instructions to tape various programmes which the girls couldn't bear to miss.

"Remember, past the pub, up the lane and you'll get to Winsford Hill," Mr. Jackson called, as the riders clattered out of his yard. "Good luck!"

"Thank you!" they all shouted at the same time.

"Now, that's what I call a real gentleman," Melanie declared.

"Yes, I can't wait to tell Rachel," Katy said. They had recently invested in a computer with Internet access at Barton Farm, mainly for Sally's bed and breakfast business. Katy and Rachel kept in touch by e-mail, which was much cheaper than the telephone, at least once a week.

By the time the riders reached Winsford Hill, the sun had broken through the mist and it was hot and sunny. The penalty for this was that they were plagued by flies, and were sorry they hadn't put fly repellent on the horses that morning.

The views from the top of Winsford Hill were spectacular, with the sun shining through the remaining wisps of mist. Several Exmoor pony mares and foals were grazing at the top of the hill, where a slight breeze gave some relief from the flies. Katy took out her camera and took a few photos of the ponies against the beautiful background view. "I wish I could paint well enough to capture scenes like this," she said wistfully.

"Why do these ponies have an anchor branded on their bottoms? Trifle doesn't have an anchor, does she?" Alice asked.

"No, only ponies from the Acland herd have that brand. I think it's something to do with Sir Thomas Acland who started this herd on Winsford Hill when the Exmoor Forest was sold in the early nineteenth century."

"You are funny, Katy! You always say that you're rubbish at school work and learning things but you know lots of things about Exmoor."

"It's easy to learn about interesting things. I know all the herd numbers of the pony herds on Exmoor, but I can't remember my times tables to save my life!" Katy said.

Although all Exmoor ponies look very similar, Katy noticed that the ponies on Winsford Hill looked slightly different from those in the Barton herd; they were generally smaller and narrower, with shorter, prettier heads than the Barton ponies. The moorland looked different from the moor Katy was used to, as well. Around Barton, it was typically close-cropped heather and rough grasses. On Winsford Hill, there were lots of small trees and gorse bushes, and a lot of the heather was old and woody. It would be difficult to gallop flat-out here the way Katy and Alice were used to doing at home.

They rode off the hill and into a wood, where the flies were so bad that Melanie dismounted, unpacked her rucksack and found the repellent, which made everyone a bit more comfortable. They had a lovely ride along a bridle path which followed the River Barle up to Withypool. The sun danced in dapples through the trees and glistened on the water. They rode mainly in silence, happily drinking in the peaceful sights and sounds along the riverbank. Near Withypool, they crossed the river and went up a track onto Withypool Hill. From there, it was a short distance to the farm where they were staying that night, with a lady called Mrs. Soames.

Mrs. Soames was one of Granfer's friends who bred Exmoor ponies. To say that she liked Exmoor ponies would be an understatement: she lived for them. She was slightly younger than Granfer, and they had been firm friends and rivals ever since Granfer had competed with his Exmoors when Rachel was a girl. Nobody on

Exmoor knew what had happened to Mr. Soames, but it was rumoured that he had left long ago because he was fed-up with eating porridge made with horse oats for every meal. With this in mind, Melanie had accepted Mrs. Soames' kind offer of accommodation, but she insisted they would take her out to supper at the pub.

Katy and Alice loved Mrs. Soames' farm. She lived in a sort of controlled, comfortable chaos. There was not a lot of difference between the house and the farmyard; many of the animals seemed to have a free range in both. Mrs. Soames took the girls to see the ponies on Withypool

Common. Katy remarked that the different herds seemed to have a different look about them.

Mrs. Soames smiled. “You have a keen eye, Katy,” she said. “Over the years, moorland breeders have encouraged certain characteristics which they admire, so now each herd has a distinctive look. I have always favoured the larger, broader, lighter-coloured ponies, myself. Your grandfather seems to like a similar type, but darker. We’re both very keen to breed the traditional type of Exmoor with a good strong jaw and a deep body. It makes them rather less attractive than these pretty little show-pony

types, which are favoured by some of the judges nowadays, but it helps them survive a moorland winter. Exmoors need large jaws to chew up the huge amount of rough vegetation they need to eat, and large stomachs to digest it all. Some of the Exmoors you see at shows are lovely riding ponies but they look as if they wouldn't last five minutes on open moorland. I remember, many years ago ... "

Katy and Alice learnt a great deal about Exmoor ponies that evening.

Contrary to Exmoor gossip about horse oats, Mrs. Soames gave her guests a hearty English breakfast, with home-produced eggs and bacon, plus homemade bread and marmalade. As if that wasn't enough, she sent them on their way with a delicious-looking picnic lunch, complete with bottles of homemade lemonade. They thanked her very much and set off up onto Withypool Common.

The early-morning mist had given way to a scorching-hot day. Melanie was glad that they had remembered to cover the horses with fly repellent and themselves with sun lotion. Bees buzzed in the heather as they skirted around Brightworthy Barrow. After crossing a stream where the horses drank, they joined the road to Landacre Bridge, which spans the River Barle. It was only eleven-thirty when they arrived at Landacre, but it was so beautiful and the pools beside the bridge looked so cool and inviting that they decided to stop for a rest and a paddle. Before long, several motorists had parked their cars for picnics, and there were screaming children and barking dogs running all over the place. Katy was surprised by how resentful she felt towards these people. Driving in a car to a beauty spot recommended by a guide book was not the same as riding through rain, hail, mist, scorching heat and flies to get there. Katy felt that she had earned the right to be there and the car-dependent tourists had not. Perhaps Melanie felt the same way because she suggested that they should move on and eat their picnic up on the moor.

After lunch, they had a lovely ride through a wood and upstream along the Barle valley to Simonsbath, passing round the Exmoor landmark of Cow Castle, an Iron Age hill fort. They stopped for ice creams in Simonsbath, and then set off along the Challacombe road to join the bridle path leading to Exe Head — an area of boggy ground where the River Exe starts.

As they approached Exe Head, they stopped and gazed at the sepia-coloured landscape around them.

"All the colours up here are the colours of Exmoor ponies: dark browns, light browns, golds and blonde highlights all mixed together. If I brought Trifle up here, she'd become invisible!" Katy said.

"You're quite right, Katy. Exmoor ponies are incredibly well-camouflaged, just as nature intended," agreed Melanie.

Alice looked down at the ground, which oozed water — like a squeezed sponge — with every step her pony took. "It's amazing to think that the water in this bog is the start of the river which runs through Exford, just a few miles away."

"Boggy ground gives me the creeps," Katy remarked.

"That's a good thing," Melanie replied. "It's always good to be wary of it. A pretty good rule of thumb is to avoid tall reeds and cotton grass, like that stuff over there, and also anything that's bright green and mossy. If you stick to these tracks you'll be OK, although — with the rain we've had recently — they're pretty wet in places. When you're on heather moorland, you'll be fairly safe if you keep to the heather and bracken because they don't like ..." Max sank, hock-deep, into a boggy patch in the track. He managed to scramble out safely. "... bogs!" Melanie completed her sentence, and the girls laughed.

The Hoaroak valley lay ahead of them. The path started off very narrow, stony and steep, and the riders had to pick their way carefully until the valley became wider. They passed an old, deserted shepherd's hut perched on a hillock and imagined what it must have been like to live in such a spectacular, isolated place. Further down the valley, they saw the Hoaroak Tree, which marks the boundary of the old Royal Forest, and then Hoaroak Cottage, another deserted dwelling.

" I feel as if I'm on home ground now," Katy said to Alice as they rode past the cottage. "I belong to this bit of Exmoor."

Alice's reply surprised Katy. "You're so lucky," she said. "I'm not really sure where I belong. I was brought up in Surrey, my father lives in London, I live on Exmoor, but I'll soon be away at boarding school. I'd love to really belong on Exmoor like you do. You can trace your family back to generations of Exmoor farmers, and everyone knows you and your family. You are the person who rides to Landacre and has a right to be there, and I'm just one of those tourists who drives in to take photos and eat sandwiches."

Katy was astonished. "You felt that too, did you? Alice, as far as I'm concerned, you belong here as much as I do."

Alice smiled uncertainly. "You're a real friend, Katy," she said. "I'm really dreading going to boarding school without you."

"Not as much as I'm dreading going to Ilfracombe without you," Katy replied. "I'm sorry I was horrid to you about it on New Year's Eve."

"That's OK. We'll always be best friends, Katy, won't we?"

"Of course we will, silly."

Chapter 7

Some You Win

Katy took Trifle to the Exford Show a few days after she came back from her holiday. She hadn't prepared properly for the show and, following an unusually cold and wet July, Trifle was already growing her winter coat. To make matters worse, Trifle's skin was covered in a layer of greasy dandruff and she had rubbed her tail while Katy had been on holiday. Granfer had told Katy that you should never shampoo a pony that lives outdoors because you take away its weather-proofing. He maintained that if ponies were properly groomed every day, they wouldn't need washing. Of course he was right, but Katy needed an instant result and only shampoo would give it. On the day of the show, Trifle shone like a new pin, thanks to the shampoo and some "coat shine" spray which Alice had lent her. Katy was very proud of her pony's instant makeover. They were bound to win lots of rosettes now.

When they got to the show, Exmoor ponies were everywhere. Trifle was frightened and excited by the whole experience. The loudspeaker was particularly scary. The other Exmoors were well-behaved, very good-looking and shining with health. The "coat shine" on Trifle was like hairspray, and it combined with the nervous sweat on her half-grown winter coat, making it stick together in spikes like a hedgehog. Katy was mortified. She was an amateur and the others were professionals. She came back from the show with a fourth rosette — there were four in the class — and a special rosette for being fifth out of six. Katy could tell that Granfer was rather disappointed by her performance, but he just said, "Never mind, Katy. You'll know what to do next year now, won't you?"

Jacko and Katy won lots of rosettes that summer, but that wasn't really important to her. She knew Jacko would probably have won them without a rider: he was that good. Katy longed to make Granfer proud of her by doing well with Trifle, and she felt that she had let him down.

Ilfracombe wasn't so bad, after all, because most of Katy's friends from Lynton School went there with her. To begin with they all stayed together, but gradually Katy made other friends, too. Her friends at Ilfracombe weren't particularly keen on horses and farming, and none of them was special in the way Alice was.

Katy had always found schoolwork hard. At Ilfracombe, she took some tests which showed she was dyslexic. The teacher told her she was very intelligent, but her brain worked in a slightly different way which made the skills of reading and writing more difficult to learn. Katy would be given extra lessons with some of the other pupils, and she would be given extra time in exams. All the teachers were very kind and understanding. They made Katy feel a bit special, not stupid as she had often felt before.

One teacher in particular brought out the best in Katy. He was a huge man with an extravagant, dark beard and twinkling eyes. His real name was Mr. Bell but his nickname was Blackbeard. He was the art teacher, and he saw that Katy was very talented. He liked one picture she had painted so much that he had it framed and entered it into a competition. It was a painting of Exmoor pony mares and foals on Winsford Hill, and it won first prize.

Katy gave the painting to her dad for his 40th birthday. He said that it was the best present he had ever had, and he hung it in the kitchen for everyone to see. Katy decided that giving a special present to someone who appreciated it was one of the best feelings in the world.

Now that she was at Ilfracombe and didn't arrive home until nearly 5 o'clock, Katy found it even harder to look after the ponies properly during the winter. Melanie agreed to keep them at Stonyford until February half term in return for Katy working at Stonyford during the weekends and Christmas holidays.

Stonyford was a lovely place to work. It was all so neat, tidy and efficient — a bit like a working toy model of a stable yard. Everything had its proper place and the horses were happy and secure. Horses love routine, company and kind, consistent handling. At Stonyford they had all these things, but with enough variety to make life fun. Katy mucked out, groomed horses, cleaned tack and helped with leading-rein lessons. In return, Melanie often gave riding lessons to Katy and a couple of other girls who helped there. Katy's confidence and ability improved tremendously. During the Christmas holidays, Melanie took Katy and Alice to several indoor show jumping competitions and Katy did really well. At one competition, Alice came first and Katy came second.

"When we see the Stonyford lorry roll up with your team inside, we know that we haven't got a chance!" a competitor's mother grumbled to Melanie.

From then on, Melanie called Alice and Katy "The Team". It made Katy feel very proud.

"There'll be no stopping us this year!" Melanie said as she drove the girls back from the last competition of the holidays. How wrong she was.

English Project . Autumn Term 2001

A Newspaper Report
About the Foot and Mouth Crisis
By Katy Squires

The foot and mouth crisis was awful. It all started on 19th February 2001, when some pigs at an abattoir in Essex were found to have a very serious virus, which causes a disease known as "foot and mouth". The pigs had come from a farm in Tyne and Wear in the north of England. From there the virus had spread to a sheep farm several miles away. Sheep from that farm had been taken to market and the disease was spread, through markets, to 96 farms all over the country before anyone knew what was happening. On Sunday, 25th February, foot and mouth disease was found on a large farm belonging to a livestock dealer near Highampton. Foot and mouth disease had spread to Devon.

This was the start of the foot and mouth crisis. Although an infected animal will usually get better, it can become so ill and the virus can spread so quickly that the Government decided to tackle foot and mouth disease with very tough rules. There was a ban on the movement of farm animals between farms or across roads within farm boundaries. All the livestock on infected farms had to be killed and burned or buried, and farmers were paid money for their slaughtered animals. Later in the year, the slaughter rules were changed to include farms next to infected farms, even if their animals were healthy. This caused a lot of bad feeling.

The latest figures are that over half-a-million cattle and three-and-a-half million sheep have been slaughtered because of foot and mouth.

Even now, when the outbreak is officially over, there are still lots of rules about the movement of farm animals. Livestock prices are very low at the moment and a lot of farmers are very poor.

Tourism has been hit, too. People were advised to stay away from farms and the countryside. Rights of way and open ground, like the moorland areas of Exmoor, were closed to the public for many months, with big fines for anyone found breaking the rules.

The foot and mouth crisis has cost millions of animals' lives and has caused a lot of suffering to animals and people. The countryside has been polluted, and farming and food supplies have been damaged. It has cost the Government over two billion pounds, and farmers and tourism many more billions. I hope that foot and mouth disease has gone for good.

Chapter 8

Foot and Mouth

The effects of the foot and mouth crisis gradually settled over Barton Farm like fog. One day the view was clear and normal, and a few days later everything had changed. Everybody was worried and afraid of what might happen. Like many farmers, Phil dreaded checking his animals each morning in case he found symptoms of the disease. The few visitors who came to the farm, like Granfer or the vet, had to disinfect themselves and their vehicles before entering and leaving. Katy had to disinfect herself before and after going to school. There were no bed and breakfast guests for five months; if they had come, there would have been nothing for them to do. Sally went no further than Lynton for her shopping. During the two months when the disease was spreading around the Barnstaple and West Down areas, Katy was kept away from school. All meetings, livestock markets, shows and point-to-point races were cancelled. Hunting was not allowed all year. Normal life on Exmoor ground to a halt.

The focal point of each day became the evening e-mail from the National Farmers Union, with news of the latest outbreaks, rules and regulations. On Katy's twelfth birthday there were 50 new cases reported in Britain, bringing the total to 890.

Horses cannot catch foot and mouth, but they can carry the virus on their hooves and bodies. For this reason, horses were not allowed to be ridden on farmland and moorland, and many competitions and Pony Club rallies were cancelled. Katy could have ridden Jacko within the farm boundaries, but Phil said that it was an unnecessary risk to keep him shod: the farrier travelled all over the Exmoor area and could bring the disease in with him. When Jacko's shoes became loose, Granfer took them off and he remained unshod until the summer holidays. Katy made sure that Trifle and Jacko were looked after, but otherwise they had a holiday out in the field from March until August.

Phil had been worried at the beginning of the year, but now — after yet another cold, wet lambing season — he was hopelessly depressed. He had too many animals on the farm — because he couldn't sell anything — he had nothing to feed them on and the farm's finances had hit an all-time low. He often wondered what life would have been like if he had gone to art school, which was what he had wanted to do. His father had told him that art was a hobby, not a proper job. The proper job for the only son of Jack Squires was to run Barton Farm, carrying on the tradition of generations. Phil had done his best to run the farm, but it felt now as if the farm were running him. His only escape from the constant worry of farming was painting, which he did whenever there was a spare moment. In the past, several guests had bought his paintings, which was an unexpected bonus. Of course, there were no guests because of the foot and mouth crisis, but Phil kept on painting. His pictures now had a desperate, frenzied quality which reflected his mood and worried Sally terribly. Phil longed to tell Sally that the farm was in an awful financial mess, but telling her would mean that he would have to face up to the reality of the situation himself. He hoped desperately for a miracle to save him from the inevitable nightmare of having to sell Barton Farm.

With no shows, Pony Club events or visits to Stonyford, Katy couldn't summon up her usual enthusiasm for anything. A telephone call at the end of April did nothing to improve her mood. The family were sitting in the kitchen watching the news when the telephone rang.

Katy answered. It was Mr. Jackson. He said that because there would be no hunting in the foreseeable future, he was going to take the opportunity to have a hip operation which he had been putting off for ages. He asked if Katy knew of anyone who would like to borrow Moon. Perhaps Katy would like to have him, or Melanie at Stonyford? If not, then not to worry because a friend of a friend was an equestrian photographer, who had taken pictures of Moon, and was very keen to borrow him. She would keep him at a livery yard with good riding facilities, so would not be too affected by foot and mouth restrictions on riding.

Katy was very excited when she put down the receiver. "That was Mr. Jackson, Dad! Guess what? He's offered to lend me Moon for a year while he has an operation! Isn't it fantastic! Can I have him? Please? Please?"

"Are you completely off your rocker, Katy?" Phil said wearily. "You can't ride the ponies you've got, so why on earth do you want another useless creature? Moon would be too much for you, anyway. Besides, I've got far too many animals on the farm and nothing to feed them on. The answer is no, and that's final."

"But Dad!"

"Katy! Not another word!"

"I hate you! I hate you!" she yelled, storming out of the kitchen and slamming the door. Then she sat on the stairs and cried. After a few minutes, Sally went to comfort Katy, and she started crying, too. Mother and daughter sat on the stairs, hugging each other and sobbing their hearts out. All the pent-up worry and disappointment of the past few months came out in their tears. In the kitchen, Phil heard them. He sat there alone, tears streaming from his eyes.

Melanie was very tempted by the offer of Moon but, like everyone, she was so uncertain about the future that she felt it would be foolish to take on any more horses. So Moon went to the equestrian photographer who lived somewhere near Tiverton, about 40 miles away.

A few months later, Mr. Jackson telephoned again. He was terribly upset. The lady who had borrowed Moon had just telephoned him to say that Moon had died in an accident. Mr. Jackson would telephone Rachel in Australia to tell her what had happened.

The animals at Barton Farm did not get foot and mouth disease, but the farm made about £15,000 less that year than Phil had estimated in the financial plan he had given to the bank. The bank manager wrote to Phil refusing his request to increase the farm's overdraft limit. The bank manager, while expressing sympathy over the unexpected problems caused by foot and mouth, asked for an urgent meeting to discuss the future of the farm. Phil tore the letter up and threw it onto the floor of the farm office.

Chapter 9

Riding Trifle

At the beginning of autumn half term, Katy rode Jacko and led Trifle over to stay at Stonyford. It was a short ride, mainly over open moorland. She carried a rucksack on her back with spare clothes, a couple of CDs and her silver photo frame. A fun-filled week lay ahead. Alice was on half term, so Katy was going to stay at Stonyford for the week. Melanie said that she would help Katy start riding Trifle that week. Katy got butterflies in her tummy just thinking about it.

Trifle was now three-and-a-half years old, and had grown into a beautiful, sturdy Exmoor pony. She was a sandy colour in the summer — much lighter than most of the ponies in the Barton herd — but her winter coat was darker brown. With better quality food than the ponies on the moor, Trifle had grown taller than the other Barton ponies. She was 13 hands exactly, and Granfer thought that she would grow another inch, to 13.1 hands.

On the Monday of half term, Katy led Trifle into the outdoor school at Stonyford. Trifle was wearing a bridle with a snaffle bit and a synthetic saddle, which Katy had got her accustomed to when she was at Barton. A casual observer seeing the pony in the school would have thought that Trifle was an experienced, reliable riding school pony. All the surroundings were familiar to her, and she was happy and relaxed, even though Katy's heart was pounding like a sledgehammer.

Melanie was in a dilemma. Putting a rider on a horse's back for the first time was always unpredictable and risky. Sometimes, horses would explode and run away, buck or rear. More often, they planted their feet on the ground and were afraid to move because of the unfamiliar weight. An Exmoor pony, with its primitive instincts for survival, would be more likely than most to go for the bucking option. The sensible thing to do would be to get Penny, her very experienced groom, to ride Trifle first. However, Melanie knew how much it would mean to Katy to be the first person to sit on her pony. It was an extraordinary moment, so for Katy — who had seen Trifle first as a newborn foal and had risked so much to own her — it would be the experience of a lifetime. Seeing how happy and relaxed Trifle was with Katy, Melanie made her decision. She would let Katy choose.

"Katy, do you want to do this, or shall I ask Penny?"

Katy wanted desperately to be the first person on Trifle's back, but the voice of reason told her that she was inexperienced and scared stiff, and should let Penny do it. "I don't know. What do you think, Melanie?"

"It's entirely up to you," Melanie said, smiling uncertainly.

"I'll do it!" said Katy, before the voice of reason could shut her up.

"It was brilliant, amazing, incredible, fantastic, mind blowing! The trouble is, no words can describe it!" Katy told Granfer on the telephone.

"Trifle was so good! First, I just lay across her back. Then I got on her properly — but without stirrups, so I could hop off quickly if I had to. She was a bit wobbly and unsure of what was going on, but she was good as gold. On the first day, we got as far as walking round the school with Melanie leading us, and today we managed to do it without being led. Perhaps tomorrow we'll try trotting. She's so sweet, and it's so odd riding her, Granfer! All you've got in front of you is a short neck, lots of mane everywhere and sweet little fluffy pointed ears at the end!"

"You make sure you keep it that way, maid! It's much better than the view of a sandy-coloured, fluffy belly and sweet little pointed hooves!" Granfer teased. "I'd love to come and see you riding her tomorrow, Katy. Do you think Melanie would mind?"

"Of course she wouldn't!"

"Right, then. I'll be over in the morning."

The next day, Granfer came to see Katy ride. He was impressed to see a very well- behaved Trifle. Katy was keen to have a go at trotting, but Melanie said it would be better to take things slowly and end on a good note.

In the afternoon, Penny rode Trifle for the first time. She was so good walking that Melanie suggested trying a little trot. Trifle suddenly exploded in a series of bucks around the school. Somehow, Penny stayed on. Katy was very glad that she hadn't tried trotting in front of Granfer. Penny worked calmly with Trifle until she was happily going from walk to trot and back again.

"Horses do sometimes get frightened when they change up a gear for the first time. It often happens when they are asked to go from trot to canter, too," Melanie explained as they walked back to the stable.

"Right. Penny can do that bit, then!" Katy said emphatically.

"She probably wouldn't have bucked with you, Katy. She likes you too much," said Penny. Katy knew that it probably wasn't true, but she thought that it was very generous of Penny to say so.

"Well, it's good that she's had a go at bucking and now she realises that it doesn't get her anywhere. Well done, Penny!" Melanie said.

On the last Saturday of half term Katy, Alice and Penny were sitting in the kitchen at Stonyford, eating a well-earned lunch. There were always lots of people booked in for rides at the weekend.

"Oh, brill!" Alice said, picking up the newspaper. "Let's see what horses are for sale this week!"

It had become a Stonyford tradition to look in the *Western Morning News* each Saturday because that was the big day for horse and pony advertisements. When Melanie had been looking for horses for the riding school, they had studied the pages in earnest. Nowadays, it was the girls' equivalent of window-shopping. They loved to look at the advertisements and imagine what the real horses were like.

"Here's one for you, Katy! Pretty cob mare. Unspoilt but green ... "

"Yuck! I'd rather not have a green pony, thanks! Brown's more my sort of colour," Katy joked.

"OK, then. How about this one? Hmmm, it sounds rather nice, actually. 'Stunning, dark bay, 7 year old gelding. 16.2 hands. Experienced hunter, dressage, cross country, show jumping. Scope to go to the top. Genuine reason for sale: £4,500 or near offer.' Sounds gorgeous. Looks gorgeous, too."

Katy took the paper from Alice. "Let's see!"

Katy's blood ran cold. She couldn't believe what she was seeing. There was a rather small, slightly blurred photo of a horse jumping a fence. The horse was Moon, and the rider was Rachel! Katy knew because she had the same photo in her silver photo frame.

Chapter 10

Life is Full of Surprises

Katy rang Mr. Jackson right away to tell him that Moon was advertised in the newspaper, but he was sure that it was a mistake. The nice lady photographer couldn't have been devious and dishonest enough to fake Moon's death and then sell him. It just wasn't possible. Eventually, he agreed to drive over to Stonyford to see Katy's photograph and compare it with the one in the advertisement.

Once Mr. Jackson had seen that the two photographs were identical, his attitude changed completely. They had to act fast.

Melanie rang the mobile number given in the advertisement and pretended she was interested in buying the horse. The man on the other end said there was somebody going to see him early on Sunday morning, so Melanie said she was prepared to pay more than the asking price, and she would like to see the horse that evening. There was no time to lose if they were to get to Tiverton before nightfall. Melanie, Alice and Katy drove in the Stonyford lorry and Mr. Jackson followed in his car. Mr. Jackson didn't recognise the address given on the telephone. It sounded as if the horse was being sold by a dealer, but the photographer who had borrowed Moon could be there, so the plan was that Mr. Jackson would wait out of sight in his car until the others were sure the horse was Moon.

The stable yard at Tiverton was a ramshackle mixture of old brick-built stables with modern low-cost stabling squeezed in between. A gum-chewing teenage girl, with bright red hair and metal studs all over her face, like designer acne, looked up from sweeping the yard as they drove in. Before they had time to say anything, she turned and walked away.

"Charming!" Melanie commented.

"Imagine what Mr. Jackson would say about

her!" Alice said, and Katy giggled.

A short, wiry man, who looked like an ageing jockey, appeared, smiling. He didn't look like a crook. "Park your lorry over there, and come to see Comet," he said cheerfully. He liked it when buyers turned up with horse transport; it meant that they were keen to buy immediately without complications like veterinary inspections.

"Can't be the same horse," Katy whispered to Alice.

"Anyone can change a name, silly!" Alice whispered back.

They walked past a row of looseboxes. Several of the horses put their ears back at the visitors, and a few tried to bite them. They stopped outside the last box. A rather thin, subdued-looking, dark bay horse stood dozing. When he saw that he had visitors, he turned to look at them and flicked his ears back. There were no markings on his face. He couldn't be Moon.

"Told you!" Katy whispered to Alice, slightly pleased that she was right but also terribly disappointed.

Melanie obviously had to pretend that she was interested. The man went into the box, tied the horse up short and took off the rugs. The horse had been blanket-clipped, and there were white hairs and sore patches on his back where a badly fitting saddle had been rubbing. Melanie ran her hand lightly over the sores.

"They're nothing," the man said quickly. "Just superficial wear and tear you'd expect to find in a horse which has seen some life." He slammed the saddle roughly onto the horse's back and the poor animal jerked his head up and flattened his ears. "Don't let his attitude in the box put you off," he continued cheerfully as he yanked up the girth. "He's totally different when he's ridden."

The red-haired girl appeared again and, without a word or a smile, got on the horse and rode him round the tiny, uneven schooling area. She rode in trainers, jeans and a denim jacket, and with no hard hat. Katy and Alice whispered to each other with glee at the thought of what Melanie would say if she were at Stonyford. Melanie was very strict about safety and wearing the correct clothes for riding. Surprisingly, the girl was a very good rider, and the horse did his best to perform well in the limited confines of the school. He jumped a high, uninviting-looking jump, cleverly dodging a pile of tyres and rusty barrels on the other side.

"I'm really looking for a hack. Could I possibly take him out for a short ride?" Melanie asked.

"Sure, but don't go too far. It will be dark soon. You can turn left-handed out of the gates there, and if you go on round the corner there's a field you can use. Would you like Sharon to come with you?"

"No, that's all right. I'll manage."

The dealer wasn't worried; he had the Stonyford lorry in his yard as security, and it was worth much more than the horse. "OK. Enjoy yourself. You'll be able to have a good gallop around the edge of the field. I expect the children would like a go, too. He's anyone's ride," he said carelessly.

"Fine. Come along then, children!" Melanie said firmly.

"What on earth is she playing at?" Alice said to Katy as they obediently followed the horse out of the yard.

As soon as they were out of sight, Melanie jumped off the horse. "It's Moon!" Her voice was triumphant. "I knew as soon as I saw him!"

"But he's totally different! And where's his new moon?" Katy said incredulously.

"The oldest trick in the book," Melanie said. "Hair dye seems to be in fashion round here. Come and look closely." Katy studied the horse's face. There was a large whorl of hair between his eyes, and his forehead was a slightly darker brown than the rest of his face. The shape of a new moon was just visible.

"You girls run and get Mr. Jackson for me," Melanie said.

Mr. Jackson was there in no time. He looked at the horse and knew it was Moon.

"Poor old chap! What have they done to you?" He said, running his hands over the horse's sore back and scars.

Mr. Jackson made a couple of calls on his mobile phone. The first was to his son, a solicitor, and the second was to the police. Then Katy and Alice were told to go and wait in Mr. Jackson's car while he and Melanie went back with Moon to sort a few things out.

Of course, the dealer denied knowing that the horse had, in effect, been stolen. He claimed that he was selling the horse on behalf of a client, but he had forgotten her name. The police arrived and studied the horse, the photos and the loan agreement. They were particularly interested in the case, because they had received several complaints about the dealer before but he had always managed to avoid prosecution. Another police car arrived with the lady photographer in it.

She claimed that there had been a misunderstanding and the horse was at the yard on livery, not to be sold.

Mr. Jackson didn't believe a word of it. He produced the loan agreement, the advertisement and Katy's photo with 'Hoof Prints Photographics', the name of the photographer's business, stamped on the back. In the face of all this evidence, the photographer changed tactics and claimed that it had been the dealer's idea. The dealer lost his temper and said a lot of things he didn't mean to say, and the police arrested the photographer and the dealer.

Finally, Mr. Jackson was allowed to load Moon into the Stonyford lorry. After what seemed like a lifetime, the children were fetched from the car where they had been waiting patiently.

Mr. Jackson said he would pay Melanie full livery for the horse for a month or so, and then they would decide what to do next.

"My specialist has told me that I can ride only if I promise not to fall off! The silly man obviously doesn't know the first thing about horses!" Mr. Jackson said.

"When Moon has been restored to his old self, we'll have to see if we can find him a really good, permanent home where he can stay for the rest of his life. I owe it to the old boy after all he's been through."

Katy decided not to tell her family about Moon until he was looking better. She didn't want Granfer to see him in such a state. In another month she would send a surprise e-mail and photo to Rachel, and perhaps Rachel would decide to buy Moon and transport him to Australia.

The following Saturday, Katy was mucking out Moon's box at Stonyford. He was being kept in the large foaling box behind the main stable yard because he had been very aggressive towards the other horses in the yard. It was likely that he had been bullied by horses at the dealer's yard, and he was going back to his old philosophy that attack was the best form of defence. Now that he was by himself, he just appeared to be bored and sad. He was tied up outside his stable, staring vacantly at the wall.

Melanie walked past on her way to the house, and paused to stroke Moon's neck. "Poor old Moon! He's existing, not living, isn't he? If he were a human, I'd send him to a doctor to be treated for depression."

Suddenly, Moon's head shot up. He pricked his ears and gave a long, rumbling whinny — the sort that horses save for special friends.

Katy laughed. "It's the threat of a doctor. Works every time with me, as well," she said.

Melanie laughed as she went to the house. Katy looked at Moon and wondered why he had become so alert all of a sudden. A few minutes later, she heard a car drive into the car park. Moon whinnied and pawed the ground.

"Melanie!" Katy called, but there was no reply from the house. "Oh, bother!" Katy muttered. She hated dealing with visitors, and she didn't want to leave Moon because he had become so ridiculously excited about something. Katy went round the corner to the stable yard.

A slim, sun-tanned lady got out of a red car. She was about 35 years old, with short, dark hair.

"Hi there, Katy!"

"Rachel!" Katy ran to her aunt and gave her a big hug. "What on earth are you doing here?"

"It's a long story. Australia was great in some ways but, once the novelty had worn off, Mark and I realised how much we missed Exmoor. It's odd, you know, but we didn't realise how important our families and friends were until we didn't have them."

"The sunshine must have been amazing, though. You're as brown as an Exmoor pony, Rachel!"

"I'll take that as a compliment, because it's coming from you!" Rachel said. "The funny thing is that we both missed the rain terribly."

"Have you and Mark come back to Exmoor for good, then?"

"Yes, we're back where we belong. I'm just so cross with myself for throwing away my dream job and my dream horse."

"Well, this is the place where dreams come true!" Katy smiled with pleasure and took Rachel by the hand. "Come and meet someone!" Katy could hear Moon working himself into a frenzy.

"Katy, I really don't want to meet anyone at the moment. I just popped in to see you and Trifle. I'm still a bit jet-lagged and I'm in no mood for a polite conversation."

"Ah, this person isn't very good at polite conversations either, Rachel. He's tall, dark and handsome, and he can't wait to meet you!"

Rachel pulled away from Katy and said in a cross voice, "Katy! Stop being so silly! I mean it! Please don't be embarrassing or I'll ... " Rachel was interrupted by the sound of galloping hooves.

"Moon!" screamed Katy.

"Moon?" Rachel echoed in disbelief.

Moon came flying round the corner.

"You see! He really couldn't wait to meet you!" Katy giggled.

Moon skidded to a halt by Rachel and nuzzled her affectionately. She hugged him and buried her face in his mane so she could breathe in his smell and hide her tears. At last she felt as if she was really home. She was happier than she had been for ages. Moon was happy, too. Rachel was the best medicine in the world for him.

Mr. Jackson gave Moon to Rachel on permanent loan. He said that if Rachel wanted to try to qualify for Badminton Horse Trials, he would give her financial backing. Owning a top-class eventer was Mr. Jackson's dream, and riding one was Rachel's dream.

On the day after Rachel returned from Australia, the sulky groom at the Exford Stables left in a huff after an argument with one of the clients. Rachel had her old job back, and she took Moon with her.

Chapter 11

Crisis

A few weeks before Christmas, Sally decided to give the whole house a really good clean. A neat and tidy place always lifted her spirits. Phil had been so depressed and withdrawn lately; it worried her terribly.

Sally didn't usually go into the farm office, but it was such a mess that she had to do something about it. Perhaps if it were tidier, Phil would be inspired to go in there a bit more.

A pile of unopened letters — most of them bills — lay in a jumbled mess on the desk, and bits of paper littered the floor. Sally bent to pick up a torn piece of paper, and something about the future of the farm caught her eye. With panic welling up inside her, Sally searched for the missing pieces of the letter and assembled them into an awful, doom-laden jigsaw. Seeing an unopened bank statement on the desk, she opened it and nearly fainted. How could anybody owe that much money to the bank? Why hadn't Phil said anything? What on earth were they going to do?

When Phil came in for lunch, Sally confronted him with the letter and bank statement. He was angry at first, and then tearful. It was awful that Sally had found out, but an immense relief to have the burden of such a terrible secret lifted from him.

In the days leading up to Christmas, Sally and Phil explored all the options available for saving Barton Farm from financial ruin, but it was too late. Eventually, and with heavy hearts, they decided that the most sensible thing would be to sell the farm, pay off their debts and try to rent somewhere nearby. Sally would get work in a hotel or a shop, and Phil could do farm work. Katy would stay at Ilfracombe College. Tom would have to abandon his dream of inheriting Barton Farm, and find a job elsewhere. All the animals would have to be sold, of course, including Granfer's treasured herd of Exmoor ponies. The bank manager agreed to lend the farm enough money to tide it over until the following autumn when everything would be sold. That would give Phil and Sally time to look for somewhere else to live.

The Squires family did not have a happy Christmas.

Katy kept Trifle and Jacko at Barton that winter so she could spend as much time with them as possible before they went to live permanently at Stonyford the following autumn. On New Year's Eve, Jacko lost a shoe in the muddy field and trod on the upturned nails. He was so lame he could barely walk. The vet had to come out to see him three times. It was likely that Jacko would be lame for several months, and he would need a great deal of care because the wounds had to be kept clean and dry. Phil was very upset when the vet's bill arrived.

It seemed to Katy that her whole life was falling apart. She had always had a firm sense of belonging at Barton. It had given her a feeling of security and stability, which she had cherished. Overnight, the rock on which her life had been built had turned to quicksand, and the whole family was sinking.

Granfer refused to talk to Dad. Tom refused to come home. Dad and Mum were miserable. Katy was afraid to say or do anything, and Rachel tried her hardest to keep the family going.

Katy's Millennium goal of winning lots of rosettes and trophies at shows seemed so foolish and unimportant now. Her only wish was that somehow they would be able to keep the farm and the ponies. Without Barton, her family would fall apart.

Chapter 12

Trifle to the Rescue

Every year, on two consecutive dawns at the beginning of February, The Exmoor District Deer Management Society conducts a census of the red deer on Exmoor. A couple of days are picked, and knowledgeable people are appointed to count the number of deer on their part of Exmoor.

Granfer was the person for the Barton Farm area. As he set off on a cold, damp, misty morning, he knew that this would be his last deer count. It would also be the last calving, lambing, drenching, de-horning, shearing, harvest and pony branding. If he thought too much about it, it would break his heart.

Phil and Sally had gone into South Molton to see the bank manager. Katy was alone in the house. She planned to watch a bit of television and then go out for a short ride on Trifle.

Katy stayed inside for longer than she meant to. She had been watching a lot of television lately; it was a good way of escaping from the heartbreaking reality of what was going on around her.

The clock in the hall struck 11, and Katy finally got dressed in jeans, short riding boots, a sweatshirt and the warm, waterproof riding coat that Rachel had given her for Christmas. As she tacked-up Trifle, she realised that Granfer hadn't come back from counting deer. He had probably stopped to chat with someone. Katy checked that the quad bike wasn't back in the shed, and then she decided to ride Trifle out towards the moor to see if she could find Granfer. Hopefully, she would meet him coming home.

At first, Katy wasn't too concerned, but after an hour or so she began to worry in earnest. The misty weather wasn't ideal for spotting deer or people. Katy started calling, but her voice seemed to be soaked up by the damp air. Trifle walked on valiantly, but Katy could feel that she was getting tired. Katy decided to call one more time and then go home for help. Her mum and dad were due back in the afternoon. Granfer may have gone home by a different route, anyway.

It was Trifle who heard him. She stopped and pricked her ears. Katy listened but couldn't hear anything. "Granfer!" she called again.

"Heeeeerrrre!" came the faint reply from a steep valley to her left. Katy kept calling. Sometimes there was an answer, and she followed the sound. Then she stopped, horrified by what she saw. The quad bike was at the bottom of a steep valley. It was tipped on its side over a stream, and Granfer was pinned underneath. Katy's knees turned to jelly, and she felt sick with fear.

"Hang on, Granfer! I'm coming!" Katy shouted as she jumped off Trifle and led her, slipping and sliding, down the steep hill.

Granfer was conscious, but he was very cold and in a great deal of pain.

"I can't feel my left leg, Katy. It's pinned under the bike. Can you get it off me?"

Katy looked around for something to tie Trifle to. Apart from the quad bike, there was nothing. She would have to tell her to stand, and hope for the best.

"Stand!" Katy said in a stern voice. She went over to the quad bike and heaved with all her might. It shifted slightly, then settled even more firmly in the bank. Granfer groaned in pain. Tears of exertion, frustration and fear ran down Katy's cheeks. "It's no good, Granfer! It won't budge! I'll have to go for help."

"No! Please don't! Use Trifle!" Granfer replied in a weird, far-away voice.

"What?"

"I can't hang on for much longer here. I feel as if I'm about to pass out. Our only hope is to use Trifle."

"How?"

"Get the baler twine on the quad bike and knot it together, several strands at a time," Granfer said with difficulty, gasping for air after each word. "Take your stirrups off the saddle and put one of the leathers round Trifle's neck. The other can join the neck one to the baler twine. It's worth a try, maid. Please try!"

Katy could see that Granfer was shivering violently.

She took a great handful of baler twine, which had been looped over the handlebars of the bike. She remembered from a television programme about emergency rescues that it was a good idea to talk to seriously injured people to keep them conscious. "I bet you won't tell Dad off again for leaving baler twine on the bike!" she said to Granfer, as she tried to wind and knot the orange strands into a rope. She knew that it was a particularly poor joke, because Granfer hardly said anything to Phil nowadays.

Trifle hadn't moved. Katy took the stirrup leathers off the saddle. She looped one round Trifle's neck and linked the other one to it, leaving the stirrups on for a bit of extra length. Her hands were trembling so much she could hardly manage the buckles. Then she tied the baler twine rope to the end stirrup and led Trifle down to the quad bike. Trifle had seen the bike many times before, but this time it looked odd and smelt strongly of the petrol which had leaked out and was floating downstream in shimmering, multi-coloured streaks. Trifle, wide-eyed, stretched her neck out and snorted at the upturned bike.

Katy turned Trifle round so that she was facing home with the bike behind her. From this position, the temptation to bolt for home would be very strong.

"Stand!" Katy commanded. She passed the end of the rope across the petrol tank of the bike and tied it to the front rack on the other side. She glanced at Granfer and forced herself to smile. He did his best to smile back. His lips had turned blue.

Now for the moment of truth! Katy went to Trifle's head and took one rein in each hand. She walked backwards slowly — trying not to fall on the slippery, uneven ground — and said, "Walk on!" in what she hoped was a firm, encouraging voice. Trifle walked towards her and then stopped abruptly as she felt the pressure of the stirrup leather round her neck. Katy took her coat off and wrapped it around the stirrup leather to prevent it from digging into the pony's neck. "Walk on!" Katy said again. Trifle walked a few paces and then stopped. Katy had an awful feeling that it wasn't going to work. "Walk on, Trifle!" The panic was showing in her voice, and she pulled hard on the reins. Trifle plunged forwards, nearly knocking Katy off her feet. There was a crash behind the pony, as the quad bike turned over. Trifle started to bound up the hill away from the noise, but she came to a shivering halt because she was tied to the quad bike. Katy was elated, but she didn't know what to do next. If she set Trifle free, the pony might bolt for home and the quad bike could run into the stream and squash Granfer. The most important thing was to save Granfer, so she had to risk it. She stroked Trifle reassuringly and said, "Stand!" again. Then she hurried to the bike and wedged it with rocks from the stream. The water was icy-cold.

Amazingly, the frightened pony stood as still as a statue while Katy got a very shaky Granfer to his feet, or rather to one foot. Granfer's left leg was soaking wet, completely numb and useless. There was no way that he would be able to walk, and the bike was too badly damaged to be of use. Katy sat Granfer on the bank of the stream and wondered what on earth to do next.

"Trifle," croaked Granfer.

"What, Granfer?" Katy could hardly hear Granfer's thin voice through his chattering teeth.

"I'll ride Trifle."

"How?"

"Bring her to the stream. I'll get on from the bank." Granfer was shaking uncontrollably.

Katy wasn't sure about Granfer's plan, but she couldn't think of a better one. She cut Trifle free from the baler twine, using Granfer's pocket knife, and put the stirrups back onto the saddle. The next task was the one she was dreading. She led Trifle into the stream and asked her to stand. The brave pony did her best to stand on the hard, slippery stones while the cold water rushed around her legs. Katy helped Granfer to lie across the saddle — using the bank as a mounting block — and then turn carefully towards Trifle's head and ease his good leg over her rump so that he was sitting astride her. Katy noticed Granfer's hands were numb with cold. She took off her socks and put them over his hands in an attempt to warm them up. Then she put her coat on him. While all this was going on, Trifle stood as still as a statue.

Trifle walked slowly and carefully. She seemed to know that she had a very fragile passenger. They followed the valley downstream a little way until they found a winding sheep track which went up the opposite side of the valley. Katy decided to go up the track and head for the nearest farm in the area, Furzewater Farm, which was owned by an elderly couple called Mr. and Mrs. Huxtable. Furzewater Farm was about 20 minutes away but Barton would take over an hour to reach. Also, the route to Furzewater was less hilly.

As they walked up the track, Granfer slumped forwards onto Trifle's neck.

"Granfer! Are you OK? Oh, please speak to me!" Katy cried in anguish. She was walking on Trifle's near side and holding Granfer steady with her hand on his leg, like she did when she was leading very small children at Stonyford so that they wouldn't fall off.

"Warm," came a muffled response.

That was how Granfer rode Trifle all the way to Furzewater; with his face buried in her bushy mane and his arms around her warm, fluffy neck. Trifle balanced her unfamiliar load very carefully as she walked beside Katy.

It was difficult navigating in the mist, which had thickened into fog. Eventually, they reached the fields above Furzewater and made their way down an old, muddy track. Katy's short riding boots filled with mud and little stones, adding to her discomfort from the blisters which had developed because she had no socks. Every step was torture.

When the farm came into view, Katy was alarmed that she couldn't see any lights on or smoke rising from the chimney. The possibility that the Huxtables could be out hadn't occurred to her before. As they entered the farmyard, a dog in a shed barked furiously, but nobody came out of the house. With an overwhelming feeling of panic, Katy shouted, "Mrs. Huxtable! Mr. Huxtable!"

There was no reply.

Katy couldn't get to the front door while she was holding Granfer and Trifle, and she was afraid to let go of them in case Granfer fell off onto the cobbled yard. The Furzewater farmyard was old-fashioned, with the house and dairy on one side, a cart linhay at the end and various livestock sheds with a hay loft above on the opposite side. In the corner was a steaming muck heap. It would be an ideal soft, warm place to put Granfer while Katy tried the doors of the farmhouse. She took Trifle up to the muck heap and eased Granfer off the pony onto the warm, smelly pile of straw and muck.

"Poo! Sorry, Granfer, but at least it's warm!" Katy said.

Granfer's eyes flickered open for a moment and he tried to smile at Katy before he sank back onto his unusual bed and closed his eyes. Katy tied Trifle to the yard gate and ran to the front door. It was locked! If only she could get to a telephone! Katy tried the back door. It was locked and all the windows were shut, too. "Oh, please! Please! Help! Help me!" Katy wailed as tears pricked her eyes. She was trying to stay calm for Granfer's sake, but it was so hard. She had made the wrong decision, and if Granfer died it would be her fault.

As if by magic, there was the faint sound of a tractor coming down the track to the farm. Katy ran out of the yard to meet it. As soon as he saw her, the young man driving the tractor stopped and got down from the cab.

"Greg! What are you doing here?" Katy exclaimed.

"I'm looking after the farm while the Huxtables are away. More to the point, what are you doing here?" Greg replied.

Katy burst into tears. Greg put his arms around her and gave her a hug. It was the best hug she had ever had.

"G-G-Granfer!" Katy sobbed. Greg's jacket smelt of silage. "G-G-Granfer's d-d-dying!"

"Sssh! It's OK, Katy," Greg said gently. "Just you tell me where he is and we'll go..."

"M-M-Muck h-heap!" Katy stammered.

"What?" Greg exclaimed. "What on earth is he doing in the muck heap?"

"I-I p-p-put him th-there," Katy replied. The explanation seemed much more reasonable to her than it did to Greg.

"Katy, this is no time for jokes!" Greg scolded.

"N-Not joking!" Katy said indignantly.

Greg ran into the yard and, sure enough, there was Granfer lying on the muck heap. He seemed to be unconscious. Katy ran after Greg, trying to explain what had happened.

Greg didn't have a key to the farmhouse, and

he had left his mobile phone at home. Leaving Katy with Granfer and Trifle, he drove off in his car to find help.

After what seemed like ages, Greg returned.

"How's Mr. Squires, Katy?" he said.

"Still breathing, but no better. I wish I could warm him somehow," Katy replied. "Did you get help?"

"Yes, they're sending the air ambulance. It should be here soon."

"Wicked!" Katy said.

"Listen, Katy. I met some people at the top of the lane. They contacted the emergency services for me. They're looking around Exmoor for locations for a new television series, and asked if they could film the rescue. I said I'd have to ask you. I don't want them to upset you, or your family."

Katy was too tired and worried to care. "Fine by me, but they mustn't frighten Trifle."

A few minutes later, three silver jeeps arrived in the yard, and several trendy-looking people got out. They unpacked cameras and equipment, and placed some blankets over Granfer. A girl gave Katy a bar of chocolate. It was just what she needed, and it tasted delicious.

It was all rather unreal, Katy thought. An hour ago, she had felt as if she and Granfer were the only humans left on the planet. Now, there were people swarming all over the place.

There was a faint, deep, throbbing noise.

"Here it comes!" one of the film crew shouted, pointing at a dark shape in the grey sky. Greg and some other men hurried to the field behind the house, where they had marked out a landing site. Katy took Trifle up the lane, away from the landing site. Luckily, the pony didn't seem to be worried by the huge, noisy monster in the sky. Perhaps she was too tired to notice.

The helicopter landed with pinpoint accuracy, and Granfer was soon flying to hospital. Katy hoped desperately that she would see him again.

Chapter 13
The Turning Point

Katy was exhausted. The film crew took her back to Barton Farm, followed by Greg driving the Huxtables' tractor and towing Trifle in a livestock trailer.

As soon as he heard about the accident at Furzewater, Phil went to the hospital to be with his father. Greg offered to do the evening farm work, and take care of Trifle and Jacko. Katy had a drink and a sandwich, and went to bed. Sally made tea for the film crew, who were trying to control their excitement. They had filmed a dramatic rescue which would feature on breakfast television news, all being well. Better still, they had found Barton Farm — the ideal location for their television series.

Katy was desperately tired, but she couldn't sleep. The events of the day kept playing on her mind. Had she been wrong to put Granfer on Trifle? Would it have been better to take Granfer to Barton? Did Greg think she was stupid? Was Trifle going to be a nervous-wreck after all her experiences? Would Granfer survive? Doubt and worry gnawed at her tired mind. She heard the film crew leave, and then Greg. Sally went outside to feed the dog and check on the ponies, and came in again. The telephone rang several times, and Sally recounted the same story in a tired voice. At last, there was a telephone call from Phil at the hospital.

"Phil! Thank goodness it's you! How's Jack? Oh, how marvellous! I'm so glad! Rachel's there with you? Good. Greg's looked after the animals, and he's coming back to help tomorrow, bless him. Yes, poor old Katy was exhausted; she fell asleep as soon as her head touched the pillow."

"I wish," Katy said to herself. She decided to get up and go downstairs to find out about Granfer. Sally had some news for Phil.

"Phil, you know those people who brought Katy back home? Well, they're from the BBC and they think Barton will be the ideal setting for a children's television series. Also, one of the men saw your paintings in the sitting room, and he really liked them. I hope you don't mind, but he's taken some photos to show a friend who's an art dealer in London. Katy's here, now. Yes, I'll tell her. She sends her love, too. Oh, and watch breakfast TV — they said they'd run the story if everything turned out all right. I'd better ring them and let them know the good news. Lots of love. Bye, then."

Sally and Katy went into the kitchen, and made hot chocolate.

"Granfer's going to be OK," Sally told Katy. "He'll have to stay in hospital for a while because he has a crushed leg, cracked ribs, shock and hypothermia."

"Hypo-what?"

"Hypothermia. It's what happens when your body gets so cold it can't work properly. The doctor treating Granfer wants to meet you. He says you saved Granfer's life."

Katy blushed. "Rubbish!" she said. "Trifle, Greg, the film crew, the air ambulance and the doctors saved his life." She had been thinking a lot about the chain of events involved in Granfer's rescue. If one link had been removed, the story would have been very different.

The following day, the story featured on breakfast television, and it became hot news. For a week or so, the telephone rang constantly, and Barton Farm was invaded by television reporters and journalists.

The film crew returned to talk to Phil about using Barton Farm as the location for a television series. It would be called 'Mousie' and it would be based on the classic tale of the Exmoor pony, 'Moorland Mousie'. The amount of money offered for the deal set Phil's head spinning. It would be enough to pay off over half of his debt to the bank. He would still have an overdraft, but the farm would be safe!

Granfer stayed in hospital for a week. The nerves in his left leg had been damaged so badly that he had to use a walking frame. Granfer's leg would never recover completely. His dancing days were over, but at least he was alive.

Katy went to see him in Porlock whenever she could. He was bored and frustrated by his lack of mobility. The news about the television crew and the possibility that there would be enough money to save the farm lifted his spirits tremendously, though.

On one of her visits, Granfer showed Katy his photo albums with old pictures of the family and the farm. Everybody in the photos looked young, happy and carefree.

"We had the best of it, Katy," said Granfer. "Farming was fun in those days; there were plenty of people to lend a hand, and the shops wanted the food we produced."

Katy turned over a page of the album. A dramatically eye-catching painting of a Fordson Major tractor working in a field — which was unmistakably Broadacre at Barton Farm — slipped out onto the floor. Katy picked it up and looked at it. Stuck onto the back was a label which read, 'Philip Squires. Winner of Southwest Young Artist Award, 14 years and under.' By the label, in her father's writing, Katy saw the words, 'To Dad. Happy Birthday. Love, Phil.'

"Wow, Granfer! This is brilliant! Why didn't you get it framed?"

Granfer sighed. "Well, it was only a child's picture, and we didn't have money for that kind of thing. I didn't want to encourage Phil's liking for art too much. He had to farm Barton, not waste his time on a hobby with no future."

"No future! Haven't you heard, Granfer? Yesterday, a man from London came to Barton and bought some of Dad's paintings. He reckons they could sell for about £800 each!"

"People in London have more money than sense, then," Granfer replied scornfully. "Why, you could buy two fat bullocks for that money!"

"Stop being grumpy, Granfer! The point is that Dad's paintings could just save the farm."

"Pah! The whole world's gone mad!" Granfer grumbled.

"Well, you could just be a bit happy for him!" Katy exclaimed, a deep sense of injustice consuming her. "I know that Rachel's your favourite because she likes horses and all the things you like, but Dad's spent his whole life trying to please you! He nearly lost the farm, but that wasn't really his fault, and now his paintings could save it. Can't you see that it would mean the world to him if you just praised him for once, rather than having a go at him all the time?" She held the picture out to Granfer. "I bet he was longing for you to frame this and put it up on your wall to show that you were proud of him!"

Katy instantly regretted what she had said. She adored Granfer and she had never spoken to him like that before. He took the picture from

Katy and sank back in his chair, looking fragile and confused.

"I think you'd better go now, Katy," Granfer said quietly.

After Katy had left, Granfer did a lot of thinking.

At the end of April, Phil received a telephone call during breakfast. He took it in the hall. When he came back into the kitchen, he was grinning like a Cheshire cat.

"I've been discovered!" he announced proudly.

"What do you mean? I discovered you years ago!" Sally joked, getting up to kiss him.

"My dear lady, you just don't understand art-speak!" Phil said in a mock-posh voice. "An art critic in London loves my work. He says it has an untamed energy which is totally unique!" He returned to his normal voice, "He wants to put some of my paintings into an exhibition, with a price tag of over £1,000 apiece!"

"That's brilliant, Phil! I'm so proud of you!" Sally said.

"Do you know?" Phil replied, "That's the first time anyone's said that to me!"

Chapter 14

Pure Gold

Gran and Granfer's golden wedding anniversary was in May, and they decided to have a party for their family and friends in Lynton Town Hall. A local pub organised the bar and a buffet supper, and they hired the same band which had played at the Millennium party and Rachel's wedding.

To begin with, everyone sat at tables talking, drinking and eating. Katy sat with Alice, who had come back from school especially for the party. It was so good to see Alice again, and Katy had so much to tell her that she was rather annoyed when the tables were cleared away and the band started to play. Katy and Alice partnered each other for the first few dances, and then a boy who was two years above Katy at school asked Alice to dance. Katy was without a dancing partner so she went to sit with Gran and Granfer.

"Having a good time, Katy?" asked Granfer.

"Yes thanks, Granfer." Katy glanced rather enviously at Alice who was obviously enjoying herself. It appeared that Katy had lost her dancing partner for the evening. Katy looked around to see if Rachel and Mark were there.

"Where's Rachel?" Katy asked Gran.

"I expect she'll be here soon," Gran replied. She didn't seem particularly worried that Rachel was missing the party. How odd.

The caller announced The West Country Waltz, and Alice's partner wasted no time in claiming her for the dance. Katy was getting her first taste of what it was like to be a wallflower at a party. It wasn't much fun. She saw her mum saying something in her dad's ear, and he came over and asked Katy to dance. It was rather humiliating, but she couldn't hurt his feelings by refusing. They were walking onto the dance floor when a voice behind them said, "Excuse me, Phil, but may I dance with your daughter?"

It was Greg! Katy's spirits soared.

"I hope you know how to do this, because I haven't got a clue!" Greg smiled at Katy as he put his arm around her. She went weak at the knees and wondered whether she would be able to dance at all. To begin with, they got into a terrible muddle and couldn't stop laughing, but by the end of the dance they were doing pretty well. To Katy's delight, Greg stayed with her for a few more dances. Then the band stopped playing, a huge cake was produced and Gran and Granfer were helped onto the stage. The cake was cut, and everyone gave three cheers. Granfer raised his hand and the guests fell silent. Katy noticed he was trembling.

"Peggy and I are very grateful to you all for turning up this evening. It means a lot to us," Granfer started in a shaky voice. "I'm not very good at expressing my feelings, but tonight I feel that I ought to. Jack Squires isn't going soft in the head; he's going to say a few things which should have been said years ago.

First, I love you, Peggy. You're the best wife any man could wish for, and I'm damned lucky that you've put up with me for all this time. I would like you all to raise your glasses to Peggy, my golden girl!"

"To Peggy!" everyone repeated as they drank a toast to her.

Gran wiped her eyes with a tissue and smiled.

"Next, I would like to say how proud I am of our son, Phil. He has been through some difficult times, many of them caused by me, but he has come through triumphant. I'm such a pig-headed old fool that I couldn't see what a gifted artist he was. I made him farm Barton when he wanted to study art. Now, it seems that his paintings are earning more than a pen of fat lambs! Well, Phil, at least I can say that I'm the proud owner of one of your earlier works!" Granfer held a framed picture above his head for the party guests to see. It was the picture Phil had given to his father many years ago.

Phil's heart leaped with long-forgotten memories. "I thought he'd thrown that away ages ago," he whispered to Sally.

"I treasure this, son. Thank you. I can't tell you how proud I am."

Everyone started clapping and cheering. Phil beamed, and his eyes filled with tears. Sally put her arm around him and hugged him.

"Now then, where was I? This emotional stuff can put a man off his stride, you know," Granfer said. There was a ripple of laughter. "Oh, yes!

Where's Katy? There you are! Come on up here!"

Katy blushed and shook her head, but Greg pushed her towards the stage. Katy climbed the stairs, and looked down at a sea of faces all smiling up at her. Granfer put his arm around Katy's shoulders. There was a commotion at the back of the hall, and several people started talking excitedly. Katy couldn't see what was going on.

"Our granddaughter, Katy, is a very special girl," Granfer continued, unperturbed. "She has made me see what is important in life. It isn't where you live or what you do or whether you win prizes in competitions. Love, family and friendships are the things that are important in life. I am lucky enough to have been blessed with all these things, thanks to all of you here tonight."

There was another round of applause, and then someone walked through the crowd of guests, followed by a camera crew. Everyone gasped in astonishment. As the man came nearer, Katy recognised him as her favourite TV presenter, Steve Harding. He presented 'Pure Gold Pets'. It was about children's pets which had done particularly heroic or funny things, and they were given a gold medal.

Steve Harding walked up the steps and onto the stage, the camera crew following his every move. Katy started to walk away to the other side of the stage. Steve Harding had come to film Granfer because of his lifelong involvement with Exmoor ponies, and she would be in the way.

"Katy Squires! Where are you off to, young lady? We've come to talk to you about your Pure Gold Pet, Trifle, the Exmoor pony," Steve Harding said. His voice sounded very loud because he was wearing a microphone. The guests began to clap, and Katy nearly fainted. She stared at the lights above the camera like a startled rabbit.

Steve Harding was used to filling in awkward silences from people who were star-struck. He turned to face the cameras while Katy recovered from her surprise. "On a cold, misty, February morning ... " Steve recounted the story of Granfer's rescue, spiced with a bit of dramatic exaggeration here and there. " ... And that is how Katy Squires and her faithful friend, Trifle, saved the life of Jack Squires," he concluded the tale of Granfer's rescue. "However, the story does not end there. I understand that due to the terrible foot and mouth crisis, Katy's family farm was facing financial ruin. Trifle's heroic rescue was reported on television and, as a result, a major film contract for the Children's BBC series, 'Mousie', has been signed. A spin-off from this is that Katy's father, Phillip Squires, has at last received the recognition he deserves for his superb paintings. In fact, one brave little pony has saved a life, a family farm business and a hitherto unrecognised artistic talent. If you will follow me downstairs, ladies and gentlemen, we will go and join the heroine herself. She can do many things but, unfortunately, walking upstairs isn't one of them!"

Trifle was standing in a blaze of lights in the entrance to the Town Hall. Rachel was holding her. The pony looked remarkably calm. In fact, she looked as if she was thoroughly enjoying herself.

"Did you know about this?" Katy whispered to Granfer.

"Afraid so," Granfer confessed, grinning. "You've got Alice to thank for it, though. She was the one who nominated Trifle for the award. It's a proper friend you've got there."

"I know," Katy agreed. "Alice is the best!"

Trifle didn't even mind when champagne corks started popping. With Rachel and Katy by her side, she wasn't afraid of anything. Glasses full of champagne were passed around, and then

Steve Harding presented Trifle with a Pure Gold Pet medal, which hung round her neck on a wide blue and gold ribbon.

"A bit more becoming than a stirrup leather wrapped in a coat!" Granfer said to Katy with a wink.

"Ladies and gentlemen!" Steve Harding announced grandly. "Please raise your glasses and drink a toast to Trifle, the Exmoor pony!"

"Trifle, the Exmoor pony!"

Other Titles by Victoria Eveleigh
Illustrated by Chris Eveleigh

ISBN 978 0 9542021 0 1

This is the first story about Katy Squires and Trifle, her Exmoor pony. On her ninth birthday, Katy finds a newborn Exmoor foal on the moor above her farm. Katy is sure the foal is destined to be hers, but life is never that simple....

ISBN 978 0 9542021 2 5

This is the third and final story about Katy and her Exmoor pony, Trifle. As a teenager, Katy faces many challenges. There are new people in her life; some become friends and others don't, but they all affect her in unexpected ways. Katy's life is full of surprises. However, the one she gets on Christmas Eve is the best of all....

FREE-LIVING EXMOOR PONIES

There are several free-living herds of Exmoor ponies on Exmoor. Each herd lives on a particular area of moorland. True Exmoors are brown, bay or dun in colour, with black points and a light oatmeal colour round the muzzle and eyes. No white markings are allowed. Although all Exmoor ponies look very similar, recognised strains have developed within the breed, which have occured because herds have been separated on different areas of moorland.

Unlike truly wild animals, such as red deer, Exmoor ponies are owned by someone who is responsible for their management and welfare. In general, the moorland pony herds live with minimum interference from people until the autumn round-up, when the herds are gathered and the foals are inspected.

At present, there are 16 free-living herds of Exmoor ponies on Exmoor:

Acland herd (anchor brand) on Winsford Hill
Exmoor National Park herds on Haddon Hill (H42)
and Warren Farm (H52)
Hawkwell herd (12) on Codsend
Moorland Herd (99) on Molland Common
Knightoncombe herd (H8) on Withypool Common
Porlock herd (100) on Porlock Common
Malcolm Westcott's herd (4) on Dunkery Hill
Tawbitts herd (H17) on Dunkery Hill
Milton herd (23) on Withypool and West Anstey Commons
Alscombe herd (421) on Deerpark and Mount Pleasant
Mr. Ford's herd (H23) on Brendon Common
Mr. and Mrs. South's herd (H67) on Blackpits
Mrs. Roberts' herd (350) on Woolhanger
Victoria Eveleigh's herd (265) on Ilkerton Ridge
Jessica Floyd's herd (387) on Brendon Common

Please do not feed free-living Exmoor ponies. Ponies which are fed by motorists learn that cars mean food, and they are much more likely to get run over than ponies which try to avoid cars and people.